The Rainforest and Other Poems

Poems by Debbie Croft

Contents

The Rainforest

The rainforest is hot and wet,
And full of leafy plants,
The vines and creepers twist and curl,
All doing nature's dance.

Tall trees grow in rainforests,
They reach up to the sky,
Where sunlight warms their branches,
As the fluffy clouds go by.

The branches of the **canopy**
Stop the sunshine peeping through,
So animals can make a home
That's cool and shady, too.

The leafy space is home
To lots of lorikeets and sloths,
And lemurs and some spider monkeys,
Butterflies and moths.

The plants that live below the trees
Spread leaves so long and wide,
It's a huge, exciting playground,
Where lots of insects hide.

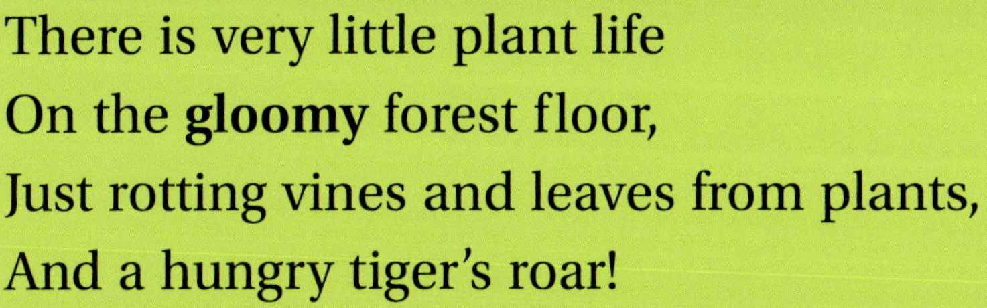

There is very little plant life
On the **gloomy** forest floor,
Just rotting vines and leaves from plants,
And a hungry tiger's roar!

The animals and plants
Have learned to live inside this space,
And help to make the rainforest
A very special place.

The Desert

In years gone by, long **camel trains**
All went across the sands,
Taking gold and silver gifts
To many other lands.

The desert days are long and hot,
There isn't any rain,
The nights can be quite cold,
Before the heat comes back again.

Some desert plants are spiky,
Some have roots that spread out wide,
Some store water in their stems,
So they can live outside.

In daytime, many animals
Will stay out of the heat,
But some of them come out at night,
To hunt for food to eat.

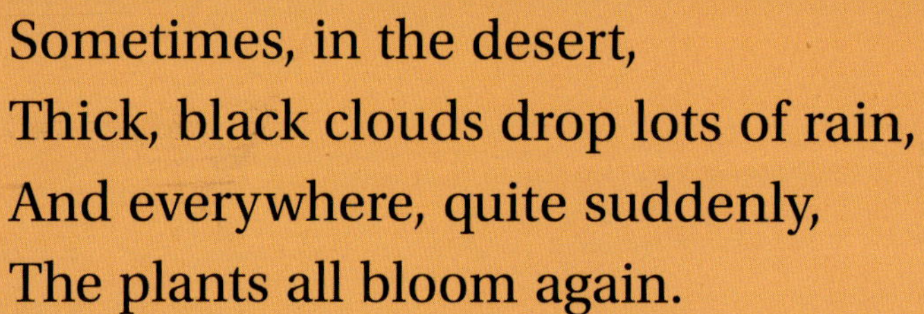

Sometimes, in the desert,
Thick, black clouds drop lots of rain,
And everywhere, quite suddenly,
The plants all bloom again.

Animals quite often
Have their young at this time, too,
The life cycles go round again,
And the desert's fresh and new.

The Savannah

The savannah is a grassland
That has trees spread far and wide,
It's a land of open grassy plains,
With little chance to hide.

The summer's very hot and wet,
Each day some rain will fall,
The winter's very long and dry,
With not much rain at all.

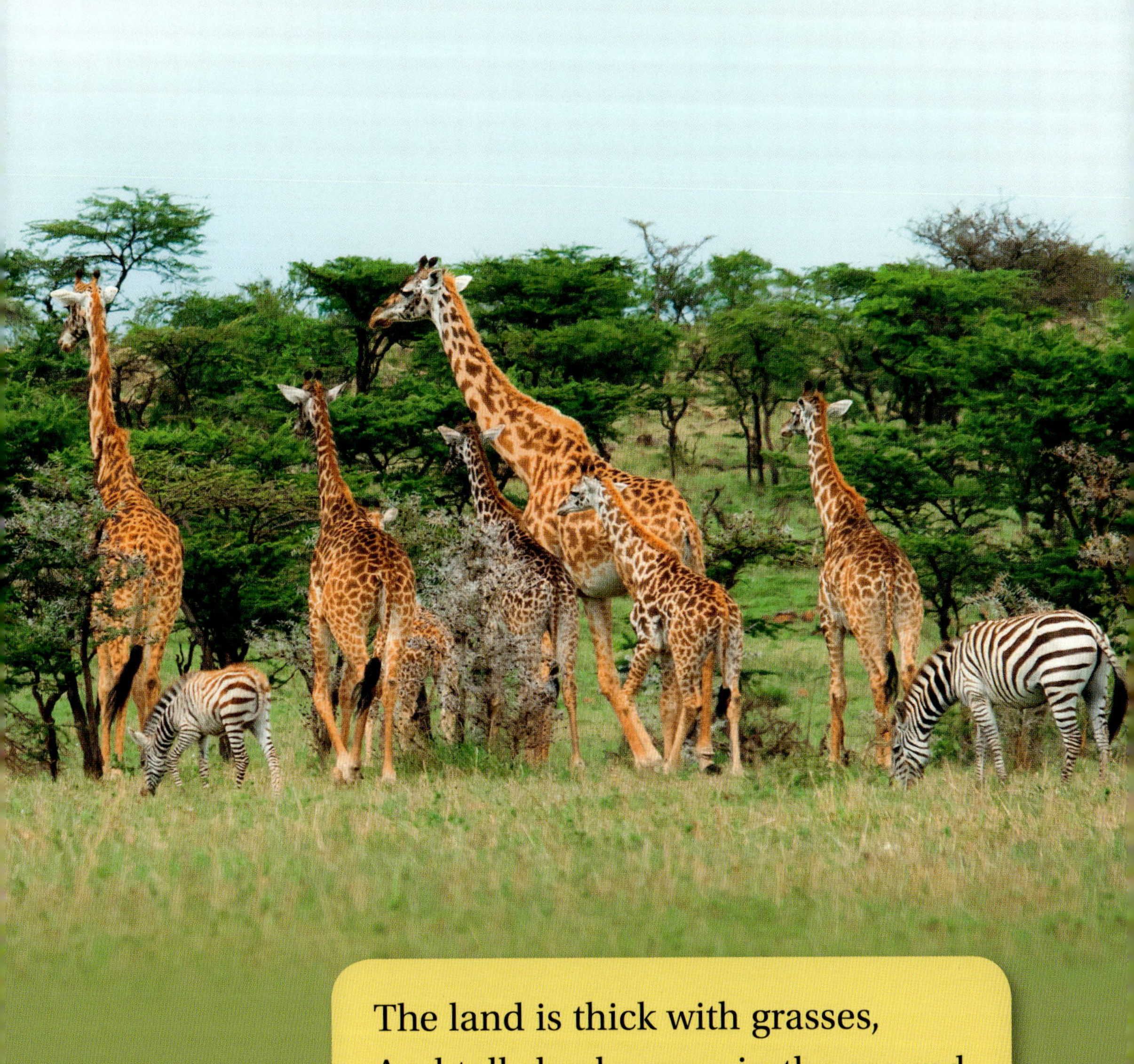

The land is thick with grasses,
And tall shrubs grow in the ground,
Lions, giraffes and elephants
And zebras can be found.

Some plants have deeper roots
And trees have bark that's very thick,
Their leaves fall off in winter,
It's a water-saving trick.

Some animals eat grasses,
Some eat leaves from way up high,
So they never have to fight about
Their favourite food supply.

But in the sky above them
Hungry eagles fly around,
They swoop down and attack their prey
That's grazing on the ground.

The Arctic

The weather in the Arctic
Is so cold with piles of snow,
There are large, flat sheets of ice,
And snowy mountains in a row.

A **glacier** is moving,
It goes slowly down the hill,
It makes a scary cracking sound,
And slides, then all is still.

There are **icebergs** in the water,
They are coloured white and blue,
There is ice above the water,
But there's more below it, too.

A polar bear is hunting
For its next delicious meal,
Waiting on the cold, cold ice
For a fat and tasty seal.

Arctic hares and foxes
Grow fur that's thick and warm,
It helps to keep them safe and snug,
In a freezing winter storm.

We must care for the Arctic,
And help everyone to know,
That this part of the world
Is such a special place to go.

Glossary

camel trains (*noun*)	single lines of camels carrying goods from one place to another
canopy (*noun*)	a layer of trees forming a roof in the forest
glacier (*noun*)	a mass of slow-moving ice and snow, close to the sea
gloomy (*adjective*)	dark and damp
icebergs (*noun*)	large masses of floating ice